# BEDTIME FOR
# BAD KiTTY

## NICK BRUEL

ROARING BROOK PRESS
New York

It's **BEDTIME**, Kitty.
Kitty does not like bedtime.

Please brush your teeth, Kitty.
Kitty does not want to brush her teeth.
Kitty wants to . . .

It's not playtime, Kitty.
It's **BEDTIME**.
Kitty does not like bedtime.

If you brush your teeth right now,
then there will be enough time
for us to read a story together.

Kitty **DOES** want to hear a story.
Kitty brushes her teeth.

It's **BEDTIME**, Kitty.
Please use the potty.
Kitty does not want
to use the potty.

Kitty wants to . . . .

It's not sing time, Kitty.
It's **BEDTIME**.
Kitty does not
like bedtime.

If you use the potty right now,
then there will be enough time
for us to read a story together.

Kitty really **DOES**
want to hear a story.
Kitty uses the potty.

It's **BEDTIME**, Kitty.
Please put on your pajamas.
Kitty does not want to
put on her pajamas.
Kitty wants to . . .

It's not run time, Kitty.
It's **BEDTIME**.
Kitty does not like bedtime.

If you put on your pajamas right now, then there will be enough time for us to read a story together.

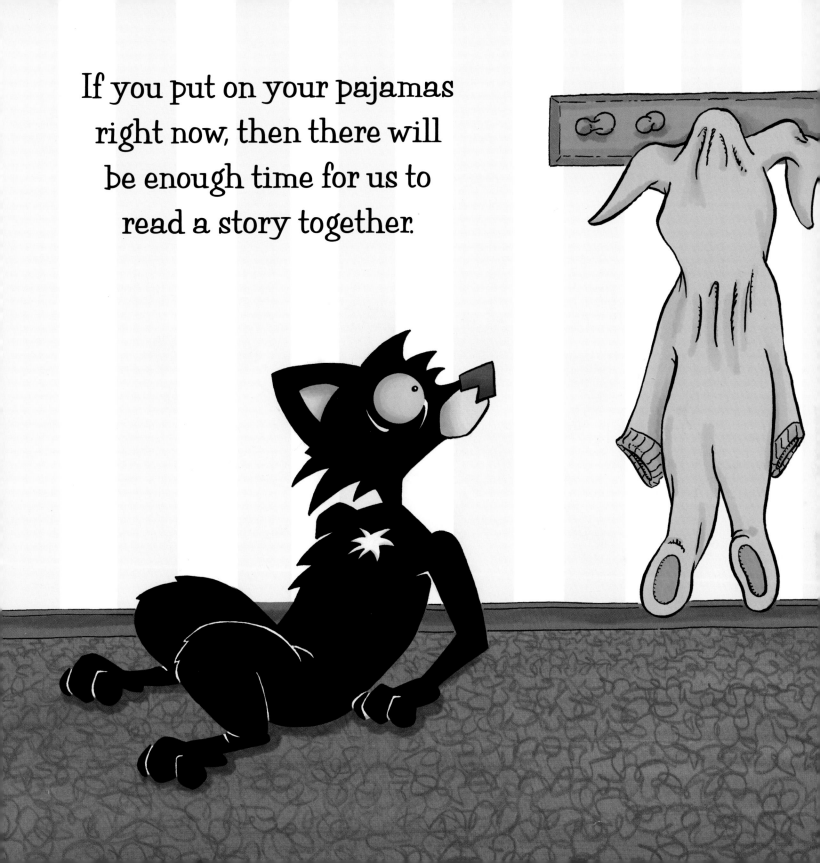

Kitty really, really **DOES**
want to hear a story.
Kitty puts on her pajamas.

Thank you for brushing your teeth and using the potty and putting on your pajamas, Kitty.
Now we can read a story together.

# Once upon a time

in a faraway land, there was a very beautiful princess who was also very naughty. She didn't like to go to bed.

She didn't like to brush her teeth or use the potty or put on her pajamas. She didn't like bedtime at all. She was a very naughty princess. But the princess DID like stories.

This is Kitty's favorite story. Kitty likes stories.

Kitty does not like